Based on the motion picture

SUPERGIRL™

AN ALEXANDER AND ILYA SALKIND PRODUCTION
ILYA SALKIND, EXECUTIVE PRODUCER
TIMOTHY BURRILL, PRODUCER
DIRECTED BY JEANNOT SZWARC
AND STARRING . . .

HELEN SLATER
PETER O'TOOLE
FAYE DUNAWAY
BRENDA VACCARO
MIA FARROW
SIMON WARD
PETER COOK
HART BOCHNER
MAUREEN TEEFY
MARC McCLURE

The Supergirl™ Storybook

BY WENDY ANDREWS

ADAPTED FROM THE
SCREENPLAY BY
DAVID ODELL

G. P. PUTNAM'S SONS
NEW YORK

ZALTAR

SUPERGIRL

BIANCA

SELENA

LINDA LEE AND LUCY LANE

ZOR-EL, KARA AND ALURA

JIMMY OLSEN

NIGEL

ETHAN

The great planet Krypton had exploded! Once the home of Superman, this spectacular empire was gone. Demolished. But there was one miracle: Argo City, part of the planet, had survived. Protected by its huge dome, this distant world had hurtled away from the deadly blast that had destroyed Krypton and was now a beautiful city honeycombed with fantastic arches, dazzling lights and lacy architecture. It was an intricate jewel, glittering but alone against the eerie darkness of Inner Space.

And here in this peacefully idyllic land, the survivors of shattered Krypton lived in contentment, inspired by Zaltar, the sculptor-artist who had founded the city. Zaltar was a magician at sculpting crystalline objects with his Matterwand, a remarkable wand which was the source of a strange, ethereal singing sound and created matter out of energy. Zaltar, however, was weary. His face was that of a man who had seen too much, done too much, and was not hopeful of bringing anything new to his life. But to Kara, a pretty young teenager, he was simply a friend whom she spent much time admiring.

"What's that going to be, Zaltar?" Kara asked him one day. She was just inside the dome which enclosed the city. It marked the edge of her world. Her mother had often warned her not to get too near the edge, but Kara wasn't thinking about that now.

"A tree, I think," said Zaltar.

"Really? What's a tree?"

"Something that grows on Earth," said Zaltar.

"You mean where my cousin went?"

"And where I think I shall perhaps venture one day soon."

Kara was startled. "I don't believe you," she said. "How?"

"In that," said Zaltar. He pointed to his homemade one-man spaceship, shaped like a sphere, that was lying nearby. Its outer casing had open segments, like the petals of a perfectly formed flower. "I'd go through the Binary Chute in that and—zip zap—I'd be gone."

Kara studied the strange ship. "You'd never leave Argo City."

"Indeed I might, Kara. Too much of a good thing here. Dulls the spirit, bores the soul. My art suffers. Here . . . watch this . . . ," Zaltar said, and as if to demonstrate his art, he produced from his pocket the Omegahedron, a small, densely packed whirling ball which was not only capable of creating all sorts of wondrous things but also supplied the

basic power that sustained life in Argo City.

"This is one of the two great Power Sources of the City," said Zaltar.

Kara was astonished. "The Omegahedron? The Guardians let you have it?"

"Not exactly," said Zaltar. "I borrowed it."

Kara couldn't hide her feeling of horror. "You *stole* it? Zaltar, they'll . . ."

"*Borrowed* it. For the afternoon, for inspiration."

Zaltar touched his Matterwand to the Omegahedron and the wand instantly became charged with flickering light. Then he touched his wand to his tree sculpture. The sculpture came alive with dancing lights!

"Kara. Kara." Alura, Kara's mother, was calling her. As Alura appeared, Zaltar deftly slipped the Omegahedron behind his back.

"Come, we are making miracles," Zaltar said to Alura. He then lifted Kara's hand and touched the Matterwand gently to her wrist. Before their eyes a marvelous glowing bracelet appeared, a bracelet made of the same material as Argo City.

Kara was delighted. And she was fascinated by what the Matterwand could do. Happily, Zaltar encouraged her to experiment with it. "Go, give it a try. Go off, let your imagination explode."

As Kara moved away, Alura confronted Zaltar. "My husband tells me you talk of leaving Argo City."

"For parts unknown. It is alas a fact."

"I can't believe it. I refuse to believe it." Alura was so absorbed in the thought of Zaltar leaving that she didn't notice Kara experimenting in the plaza nearby, making all sorts of kaleidoscopic light drawings in midair and the most amazing sounds with the Matterwand. She didn't notice either as Zaltar tapped the Omegahedron with his toe, rolling it away, and once again cleverly preventing her from seeing it.

"Zaltar," Alura continued, "you founded this City! It's

yours. We were all just refugees from Krypton when you . . ."

"The Guardians have all the responsibility now," Zaltar interrupted her. "I'm an artist. I can't limit myself to Argo City. You and Zor-El have a life here, you have Kara and you have each other. Me? I have . . . I have a headache."

While Alura and Zaltar were completely wrapped up in their discussion, Kara, alone in the background, was modeling a spiky, insect-like creature. Suddenly she found the Omegahedron coming to rest on the ground beside her. She didn't stop to wonder how it got there. She simply picked it up and touched it to the spiky creature. The creature suddenly flicked its wings and came to life, unnoticed by the adults. Kara laughed as the magical creature took off from

the ground and started flying in circles around her head. It glittered as if it were made of diamonds!

But now the insect was flying closer and still closer around Kara's head, buzzing angrily. Kara's look of delight turned to fear as she tried to shoo the thing away. It flew off . . . toward the thin membrane that enclosed the City . . . then unexpectedly, suddenly *into* the membrane, tearing a ragged hole in it! With a giant WHOOSH all the air in the City started to rush out the hole. And the Omegahedron was sucked instantly out the hole by the force of the wind, lost to the reaches of outer space!

Zaltar, Alura and others, distracted by the commotion, rushed up, to see Kara being swept along, horribly, helplessly toward the hole. Zor-El, Kara's father, was among the crowd.

"Father! Help me . . ." Kara screamed, dropping the Matterwand to the ground as she grabbed the ragged edge of the membrane. She dangled half in, half out of the dome, suspended in the turbulence.

Zaltar grabbed the fallen Matterwand from where Kara had dropped it, touched her with it, and Kara was instantly held fast. Zaltar, Zor-El and Alura together pulled Kara back inside, struggling against the violent rush of wind. Zaltar then touched the Matterwand to the tear in the membrane and sealed the hole with the crash of a brass choir. The wind died.

Alura was concerned for her daughter. "Kara . . ."

"I'm alright, Mother."

Zor-El was angry and looked sharply at Zaltar. "You took the Omegahedron."

"Correction: I *lost* the Omegahedron," said Zaltar.

"No . . . I did. I . . ." Kara couldn't finish.

"Silence, Kara," said Zaltar.

"No matter who," said Zor-El, "without it this City cannot survive."

"Our lights will grow dim," said Alura, "and the very air we breathe so thin that in a matter of days . . ."

As others converged on the scene, alerted by the catastrophe, Kara backed away. She was terrified by her father's anger, her mother's fear and Zaltar's shame. But most of all she was terrified by the enormity of what had happened. No one noticed as she slipped away to Zaltar's space vehicle and quietly climbed into it through the hatch.

Outside the space vehicle Zaltar and Zor-El continued arguing.

"But I can find it. I can chase the Omegahedron in my ship . . ." Zaltar was insisting.

"Like a coward," said Zor-El. "While the rest of us are doomed to stay here in our beloved city and perish. This is our universe and now you've destroyed it. With a childish game!"

The conversation stopped as everyone turned toward the sound of a deep rumble coming from the space vehicle. Kara had enclosed herself within its curved petals and was floating toward the Binary Chute. She was frightened and sad, but determined. Everyone raced to the edge of the level, but the spaceship was now receding into the abyss of the

Binary Chute, forever out of reach. There was a deep pulse of light, like a silent explosion below them.

"She'll be killed!" Alura screamed, reaching out for Kara.

"No! She *won't*!" Zaltar said, resignedly. His eyes were wide. Sweat beaded his brow. "She's safe, I promise. Safer than we are . . . through the Binary . . . through the Warp . . . into another Register . . ."

"What? Another *what*?" Zor-El shouted.

"A register, a pathway from inner space to outer space . . . gravitational radiation," Zaltar said.

"Then she will never be the same! Ever again!" Alura cried.

"At least *she* will be alive." Zor-El's eyes pierced Zaltar.

"My fate is sealed," said Zaltar. "I've lost the Omegahedron . . . I must be sent to the Phantom Zone. Your suffering will be short . . . mine forever . . ."

Kara was being tossed about, the space vehicle buffeted by strange forces, then suddenly steadying and accelerating. Quickly, Kara's sphere expelled from Argo's underside and the huge domed city was suspended in a black void. Then, like a speck of dust, the tiny vehicle was sucked by invisible currents into a great vortex. Swept away!

It was a whirling mass! A cyclone of such savage intensity that Kara's sphere seemed to stand no chance against the fantastic eddies and violent updrafts. Kara's face was a blur until she hit the Eye of Inner Space. Unexpectedly, everything slowed down . . . like a dream . . . and then brightened. Then Kara spotted it. The Omegahedron floating in dazzling light! If only she could lock on to its track. BUT THE SPACE VEHICLE WAS LOCKED IN A TIGHT, UNCHANGING RELATIONSHIP TO THE OMEGAHEDRON.

Suddenly in the distance, Kara saw a thin, white horizontal line of gravitational radiation. It gradually expanded until she was in a zone of extraordinary warped white light which engulfed the space vehicle. She was crossing through the Register from inner to outer space. Still chasing the Omegahedron, Kara emerged from the Register into a dark green limbo. The atmosphere thickened around her until it was the sea. She was heading toward the light above, following the Omegahedron through eternity.

On Earth, a man and woman were picnicking by a lake. They were not your average couple. Selena, strikingly beautiful, was a vicious small-time witch whose ambition was to control the world. She was not concerned that this particular goal had eluded or eliminated almost everyone who had ever gone for it.

Selena took her frustration out on her boyfriend, Nigel, a fussy, pushy high school math teacher and part-time practitioner of black magic, who was now preoccupied with looking through his wicker hamper containing wine, lobster, French bread, mayonnaise sauce and tarot cards. Selena was more interested in power than food.

"It's such a pretty world. I can't wait until it's all mine. But how to get it all while I'm still young enough to enjoy it," Selena was saying.

"The only way to rule the world is to become invisible, my pumpkin."

"Invisible?"

"Yes, I know how to do it. But you're impatient. You want everything yesterday. It takes a lifetime to learn all the secrets of black magic."

"Nigel, how long have we been together?"

"Months, my darling."

"Then why does it seem like years?"

Suddenly something burst from the lake, whistled straight up into the air, and hung there. It was the size of a softball. It dropped as Selena and Nigel dove for cover. Crash! Into the mayonnaise sauce! Half in, half out sat the Omegahedron power source from Argo City.

"Holy cow . . ."

Selena kneeled down before it. Its eerie glow made her face look more sinister. "Immortality be upon this one," she said. "This is POWER, sent to me, Selena, from the heavens. This is it, Nigel! No longer will I be a lower-echelon witch!"

Selena, as if possessed, removed the Omegahedron from the mayonnaise sauce. Then she turned to Nigel. "I've just outgrown you, Nigel."

"You can't treat me like this. I can send you back where you came from, Selena. If it wasn't for me, baby, you'd still be reading tea leaves at Lake Tahoe!"

Selena ignored him and headed for her Cadillac, carrying the mysterious Omegahedron close to her. It turned on the car radio! The closer she put it to the radio, the more volume came through. She heard the announcement: The President confirmed reports that Superman has embarked on a special peace-seeking mission to a galaxy several hundred trillion light years from our own. The President declined to comment on the length of Superman's absence from Earth, but a reliable source in the State Department said, "I don't care how fast he flies, these things take time."

Selena moved the Omegahedron toward the ignition . . . and the engine sprang to life. Nigel, approaching Selena with the car keys dangling from his fingers, froze in his tracks as Selena sped away in a cloud of sand.

In slow motion Kara sprang free from the surface of the water, and landed, stumbling, unsteady, unsure on a nearby stretch of ground. She looked around. She was surrounded by trees, huge, magnificent and real, like the ones Zaltar had yearned to see. This was a strange new world. She looked down at herself. She was wearing a red and blue costume like her cousin Superman!

Where was she? Who was she? What was happening?
SHE WAS ON EARTH!

Kara was fascinated by this strange world and startled by her own powers. She picked up a stone and to her astonishment, crushed it to powder in her hand. She looked at a wild flower and at the touch of her HEAT VISION it miraculously sprang into bloom.

She gazed down again and was amazed to find she was a yard off the ground! Suddenly she shot upward into the blue sky, high above the earth. She zigzagged, made full stops and sudden starts. Over the water, over the countryside, everywhere, she made loops and rolls and swoops and circles. She was full of joy.

A furious Nigel, trudging home cursing Selena as he struggled with the picnic basket, suddenly heard a low-pitched whooshing sound from above. He looked up at the sky and now saw the most astounding sight—a caped figure in that familiar red and blue uniform streaking across the skies.

"Superman?"

Supergirl continued her aerial ballet, over the mountains. She bounced from rock to rock, and laughed with sheer delight. But at last she came down to Earth, remembering her responsibilities and her mission here. As she stood at the edge of the sea alone, truly alone, a resolve came upon her: the Omegahedron *must* be found.

Selena, triumphantly wiping the last bits of mayonnaise sauce from her newly found source of power, arrived home.

"Home!" she muttered as she tripped over some remnants of a railroad track. That was easy to do, since Selena lived in a ghost train on the remains of a railroad track in an abandoned amusement park. "This would be the worst house in the neighborhood," she laughed sarcastically, "if there *was* a neighborhood."

Inside the windowless place was cluttered with old furniture, fun-house mirrors, a painted canvas backdrop of a grotesque Fat Lady, a spooky old fortunetelling machine in the shape of a gypsy hag and numerous other tributes to Selena's decorating skills. It was a nice place to visit but . . .

"Beeeeeeee-an-ca! I'm home! Show your face, darling!"

Selena swept in. She rummaged through all the junk on

her desk and at last found the Coffer of Shadow, a hatefully ugly lead box. It was just the right size to contain that glowing Omegahedron.

Bianca, Selena's best friend and an evil-looking spike of a woman, greeted her. "They turned off the hot water again. I'm gonna have to kill somebody at the DWP. I figure the only way we're gonna pay our bills around this dump *next* month is just go ahead and, you know, start our own, you know, coven. I was reading in this book, *The Witch's Guide to Heaven and Hell*, that if you like *start* a coven yourself then you can charge five bucks a head minimal admission. What's in the Coffer of Shadow over there? Where's little Nigel?"

"Nigel, my dear nasty Bianca, is history. The Water Department is history. The world is at last our oyster."

"You, uh, wanna maybe let Bianca in on this unexpected good luck we're having or whatever it is?"

"I have been chosen. I think the Powers of Darkness at long last may have come to their senses."

Bianca didn't quite follow Selena's drift, but she started to catch on that night when Selena threw a party. It wasn't your average affair. Selena, perched on a garish, carnival throne a bit above the proceedings, a glass of wine smoking in her hand, watched some truly marginal types milling around.

"I simply cannot control the world without help," she

told Nigel. "And good help is almost impossible to find these days. All the really capable witches and warlocks have been hired away by the competition."

"Control the world?" gasped Nigel. "That's your plan? I don't like this, Selena. I don't like this at all." Nigel stared at the guests. "Who do we have here? Weirdos, misfits, eccentrics, wrinkly little wretches from the yellow pages, munching your treats and drinking your wine. And speaking of competition, after you left me at the lake, I saw something that should worry you greatly if you're really serious about this world domination thing. It was blue and red and it knew how to fly."

"I have the *Power*, Nigel," Selena retorted. "Get that through your head. Selena is through worrying. The shoe is on the other foot, and now it's their turn to worry." As if to prove her point, Selena focused her eyes on a drink that a young girl was holding. As the girl started to take a sip, a scorpion rose from the foam and jumped into her mouth! The girl rocketed to her feet, clutching her throat as the other guests watched in horror. Suddenly the girl was on her head, spinning like a top!

"Stop it, Selena. That's not fair. Pick on me," Nigel urged.

"I like it. Very different." Bianca was into it. She was even more into it when the girl plummeted down on top of her.

"Whew . . . Excuse me," the girl let out.

"Hey, no sweat."

"Get out of my house, Nigel. And don't come slithering back," Selena ordered.

"I'm the only one who can save you from yourself, Selena. You need me."

"Like an Eskimo needs a lawnmower, kiddo."

Nigel had had it. He turned and left the party in disgust at the same time that Selena exited the room.

There was silence as everyone at the party had witnessed the altercation. But Bianca broke that up. "Come on, folks, the show's over. Let's party."

It was morning, lush and beautiful in the forest where Kara, now Supergirl, enveloped in her red and blue uniform, had fallen asleep. Suddenly Supergirl opened her eyes as a spherical object crashed overhead, rolling to a stop five yards away from a clearing.

"It's the Omegahedron!" Supergirl thought. But only for a moment. It was a spherical object of the earth, a softball.

There was another sound of bushes crackling. Before Supergirl could react, Lucy Lane broke through the foliage. She was wearing a Midvale School uniform and she was so intent on retrieving the softball that she didn't notice Supergirl sitting there.

"I got it!" Lucy shouted, and she was gone.

Supergirl parted the bushes and saw a softball game in progress on the Midvale School campus. Lucy was one of the players. Watching the game were schoolgirls dressed in uniforms of skirt, blazer and white knee socks.

As she watched, Supergirl got an idea. She would become a student here. Slowly breaking into a run, Supergirl moved with graceful purpose through the forest, gradually changing from the golden-haired Supergirl in her red and blue costume to a girl with mousy brown hair wearing the ordinary Midvale School uniform. She had become Linda Lee, mild-mannered student.

Linda, a rucksack slung over her shoulder, walked up the school driveway and into the building, passing Myra the school bully, who was, as always, accompanied by her toady spy, Muffy. Myra spoke in a loud voice. "Geez, another barfy new student. They're really scraping the bottom of the barrel these days."

Linda ignored the remark.

On the second floor, she entered the office of the registrar, Mr. Danvers. Mr. Danvers was busy taking aspirin. He got up and began a slow, menacing circle around Linda. "I have never laid eyes upon you, have I, young lady? Who on earth are you?"

"On Earth I'm Linda Lee."

"Where's your letter of recommendation?"

"Letter?"

Suddenly Mr. Danvers' door burst open and Nigel appeared. From the way he was complaining, Linda realized he was a teacher at the school. As Nigel distracted Mr. Danvers, leading him out of the room, Linda wasted no time. She located a typewriter and some blank paper and at SUPERSPEED pounded out a letter which she managed to slip into the "K" file just as Mr. Danvers was returning.

She coyly suggested to Mr. Danvers, "My cousin probably wrote you. Clark Kent."

Mr. Danvers found the letter in his "K" file. "Dear Mr. Danvers, I am writing to you on behalf of a very special young lady, an orphan . . ."

Supergirl was accepted as Linda Lee at Midvale. Mr. Danvers took her to the dorm to meet her roommate, Lucy Lane.

Nervously Linda introduced herself, "I'm Linda Lee."

"Hi. Lucy Lane."

Mr. Danvers piped up, "Lucy Lee, this is Linda Lane."

"No, it's not," said Lucy.

"What?" Mr. Danvers was bewildered.

"She's Linda *Lee*," Lucy explained. "And I'm . . ."

". . . Lucy *Lane*," Linda finished.

"You *know* each other?"

"We just met," said Linda.

"But we've known each other for years," said Lucy smiling, amused at Mr. Danvers. "Haven't we, Linda?"

"Gee, I don't think I . . ."

Mr. Danvers piped up enthusiastically. "Of course! *The Daily Planet!* Linda's cousin works there and so does your sister . . . uh . . . what's her name . . ."

"Lois," said Lucy.

Linda started to look around the room. This was her new home. Some of it was so strange. The rock posters on the walls, the stereo . . . they didn't have these things in Argo City.

After Mr. Danvers left, Lucy asked, "So who's your cousin?"

"Clark Kent."

"Clark Kent. Are you putting me on?"

"Do you know him?" Linda was equally incredulous.

"Do I know him?" Lucy repeated. "Does my *sister* know him? Now that is the big question."

Lucy winked slyly, but Linda didn't understand. "Well," said Linda, "if they work at the same newspaper together, I guess she must. Is this where I'll sleep?"

"It's your bed," said Lucy, "but we don't sleep much around here. Nonstop excitement in this dorm. All the real dementoes are sent here. Whatcha staring at?"

Linda couldn't take her eyes off a gigantic poster of Superman on the wall. "Do you know *him?*" Linda asked.

"Superman. Sure. My sister's got something special going with the big guy. Say, where's your stuff? All you've got is a little bag. You have a fire at your house or something?"

"I have money to buy more. I haven't had a chance . . ."

"Listen, me and my motor-mouth, huh. You can borrow any of my clothes any time you want."

"Thank you," said Linda. "You're very nice."

Then Linda couldn't help herself. She reached out and touched the Superman poster with just her fingertips.

"A real hunk," said Lucy. "I'll introduce you some day if we wind up getting along."

L ucy and Linda more than wound up getting along; they became good friends. Lucy didn't always understand Linda; in fact, sometimes she thought Linda was so different from any other girl she knew that she must be from another planet. But that didn't stop Lucy from liking her.

And Linda was trying to enter into life at Midvale as best she could. She had to do everything the other girls did. Including playing field hockey. She had to dress in the Midvale green and white gym outfit, get out on the field and *play!* But Linda had her own way about things.

One day, during a game, Linda saw Myra deliberately trip Lucy. Linda rushed to help Lucy up. "She did that on purpose," Linda said.

"Absolutely. She's a creep."

The team, with Myra in the lead, headed back toward them, and Myra slapped the ball directly at Lucy. It was going to hit her! Linda ran in front of Lucy and the ball hit Linda and shattered!

The playing stopped. All the girls started picking up little pieces of the ball.

"How'd you do that? You okay?" Lucy asked Linda.

"Sure. I think."

Myra and Muffy looked at each other in shock and then stared at the pieces. Their faces were a combination of stupidity and evil.

On the way to the locker room, Lucy warned Linda. "Keep an eye peeled for Myra. She's out to get *you* now. She hates anybody who's not afraid of her."

Sure enough, inside the locker room, as Linda and Lucy stepped under nice warm showers, Linda's SUPERHEARING and X-RAY VISION alerted her to the sound of Myra next door fooling with the plumbing!

"I just can't *wait* for their screams," Myra said to Muffy as she took a huge wrench and started to shut off the cold water valve.

"But Myra, why don't you shut off the hot water and give them an ice bath? If you shut off the cold, you'll scald them." Muffy seemed worried.

"So they lose a little skin," Myra said. "Serve 'em right."

Myra pulled on the wrench as Linda shot a beam of HEAT VISION through the wall. The wrench glowed red-hot in Myra's hand. She dropped the wrench with a cry of pain. The pipe sprang a leak, drenching her. More pipes sprang leaks!

"The pipes!" cried Myra. "They've gone crazy!"

Soaked to the skin, Myra and Muffy ran out of the plumbing room past a satisfied Linda and a slightly bewildered but amused Lucy in the showers.

Linda's powers were her ally but also her problem. She had to be careful in the classroom. She knew more than she realized. When Nigel asked her to solve an equation in computing class, she was able to come up with an answer of five billion, two hundred seventy-one million, nine thousand and ten, the correct answer. She astonished everyone. And when a tremendous rattling of the classroom windows shook the room, Linda's SUPERHEARING tuned into that special frequency . . . the Omegahedron! And her X-RAY VISION saw Selena and Bianca in a car near the school. What did that mean? Zaltar's bracelet, ever around her wrist, pulsed excitedly with heat and energy. Then as Selena and Bianca drove off, the rattling stopped and the bracelet grew dim again. It was hard for Linda to keep in mind that she was supposed to be an ordinary schoolgirl with ordinary interests.

But it was hard to have ordinary interests when you didn't know what they were. Linda didn't know what to make of Lucy's offer to pierce her ears one afternoon when they were hanging around the dorm after hockey practice.

"You want to do *what?*"

"Pierce your ears. You know, like in I take a needle and heat it up and we dab on some alcohol and zap! Then all the guys go crazy."

"Because I have holes in my ears?"

"You're putting me on, right? I can't figure you out, ya know? Where you going for the weekend?"

"Nowhere."

Linda went to their bureau and started to tidy up. She came across one of Lucy's bras. What in the world was *this?*

Lucy kept talking. *"Nowhere?* Well, you can't stay here. It'll be too depressing. I mean, like a tomb."

"Why?"

"*Why?* What, were you born yesterday? Memorial Day. Three-day weekend. Come on home with me. I live like five miles away so we can still hang out at Chicken City and plus I got this guy coming up to see me from Metropolis . . . hey, he knows your cousin, Clark. Jimmy Olsen's his name. I think he loves me."

"Thanks," Linda said, "but I'll just stay here and study and get organized."

"Organized? What's there to organize? Your side of this room looks like a monastery. No posters, no family pictures . . . my side, on the other hand, gives new meaning to the word junk."

"I could organize your drawers," said Linda. Still puzzled, she held up the bra. "Where do you usually put this?"

"On me, of course," said Lucy.

"On *you,*" Linda said, relieved. "Just as I suspected."

Now Lucy was puzzled. "Linda," she said. "Are you for real?"

Linda didn't answer. She put Lucy's bra back in the drawer and closed it. Perhaps during Memorial Day Weekend, whatever that was, she could learn more about everything. She'd be alone in the dorm. In a way, she was alone right now. A stranger from Argo City, hoping desperately to find the Omegahedron, but finding instead information about oddly-shaped garments and putting holes in ears.

Selena was in love. His name was Ethan and he was very big on weed and insect control. He was a landscaper, and owned his own business, Ethan's Mother Earth Weed and Insect Control, specializing in 23½-hour service. Selena had seen him outside the Midvale School where he was working.

And now this muscular, sexual animal in his rugged tee-shirt, aviator sunglasses and chewing gum stood at the entrance to the ghost train, about to knock on Selena's door. "This," he thought, "has got to be the ultimate dump."

Inside, Selena was concocting a love potion. "My prince is coming," she said.

"That's because you invited him here to look at your dead lawn," said Bianca.

"Wait until he drinks from this potion I made from a spider stuck inside two shells of a nut," said Selena. "He who drinks this shall be in love with the first person he sees. For one full day. Ah, I hear the doorbell!"

Selena, leaning seductively on the jamb, opened the door.

"You rang?" she asked.

Ethan lifted his sunglasses for a better view. "Yeah. I'm looking for a person called Mrs. Selena."

"You found her, lucky boy. *Entrez!*"

Ethan sauntered inside. "How you doin'?"

"Having a ball," said Bianca.

"So where's the lawn at?" he asked.

"It died," said Bianca.

"I was hoping we might get to know each other a little before we talk business," said Selena.

"I'm kind of a private person, you know," said Ethan. "I do my job, I go home . . ."

"To your wife?" asked Selena.

"No. At this present moment in time I am currently enjoying a single status in my personal life."

Selena instantly offered Ethan a beer spiked with her love potion. "Cheers," said Selena, as Ethan drank.

Ethan wandered around the room, trying to digest the ultra-weird decor. "This is a house?"

"Of course it's a house," Selena responded. "The bedroom's over there, she said pointing to an awesome chamber done in breathtakingly bad taste and conscientiously maintained like a pigpen. Selena's huge bed, under a pointed canopy of zebra skin, was elevated in the center of the room like an altar. It could be reached by a ladder. Perpetually unmade, its zebra-skin cover draped the floor. On one wall of the room, there was a huge pink-framed mirror shrouded with a thick veil.

Ethan didn't quite know what to make of it all, but it didn't matter because after a brief conversation about alkaline soil and cherry houseplants, he collapsed.

The doorbell rang. "If that's the blasted vacuum cleaner salesman again . . ." Selena said.

It was Nigel, dressed in a skin-tight gray vinyl jumpsuit with chrome zippers.

"Nice suit," Bianca said, not letting him inside.

"You girls are rank amateurs playing with fire," Nigel said ignoring her, his foot holding open the door. "You used to listen to me. Now some stupid little glowing gyroscope lands in your mayonnaise sauce and all I am is yesterday's news."

"Take a hike, Nigel," said Selena. "And a word of advice. If I had your skin problems, I'd stop bothering people, put a bag on my head, and go live under a bridge." She slammed the door.

Nigel, vain about his complexion, was thrown completely off stride. "My skin? It's perfection." But when he caught his reflection in the mirror on the ghost train door, he recoiled in horror as his face suddenly erupted in ugly red blotches.

Meanwhile, Ethan had split. Hallucinating from the love potion, seeing spiders and skeletons in his path, and out of his skull himself, he had staggered out the back door of Selena's house.

Selena was in a rage looking for him everywhere. "He'll spoil everything! Whoever he sees first he'll love with all his heart!"

"What, for a day tops, right?" said Bianca. "He was too young for you anyway, you know?"

"No, I do *not* know!"

Selena spun around furiously, suddenly confronting her own terrible image in her ugly pink-framed mirror. *She locked eyes with herself* and asked, *"Where is he?"*

In response an astounding thing happened! The surface of Selena's pink mirror crackled, buzzed, radiated purple light for an instant and then dissolved into . . . a weird viewing screen . . . A MAGIC SPYGLASS ON THE WORLD!

The "world" right now was Ethan. He had stumbled into and was crawling away from the amusement park. There was no sound.

"What's happening? Why is my mirror doing this?"

Selena pounded on her mirror. The mirror had gone to static and scrambled lines. Selena spun around, threw back her rug, and ripped open her secret compartment where she kept the Coffer of Shadow. "It's stuck! It's *growing!* The power inside is controlling the mirror!"

Selena managed to pull out the Coffer of Shadow. It was definitely larger. And it was glowing! The mirror crackled! The picture cleared up! There was Ethan, staggering down the middle of a highway outside of town as cars whizzed past him.

Supergirl had been flying all morning, coasting high above the tiny hamlet of Midvale, her X-RAY VISION trying desperately to locate the precious Omegahedron. The special frequency was suddenly audible. She reversed direction, flying upside down for an instant, then hovering. The sound faded. "Where? *Where?*" she asked. But there was silence except for the rush of the wind.

Suddenly Supergirl spotted a building that had the word *chicken* in its sign, Popeye's Famous Fried Chicken. Could this be the Chicken City Lucy had told her about? Supergirl swooped down from the skies, flew into a large pipe and emerged on the other end as Linda Lee. She started to cross the road to Popeye's. Through the window, Lucy caught sight of her. There was a crowd of teens with Lucy, listening to rock music and eating fried chicken.

As Linda entered, Lucy ran over to her. "Linda babes," she whispered. "That's Jimmy Olsen, the cub reporter from Metropolis. He's the one with the camera dangling around his neck. I was right. He loves me more than life itself . . . And hey, look at that dingleberry! Hey, you, space cadet, get outta the street." Lucy had spotted Ethan reeling in the center of traffic down Main Street.

"What's his problem?" Linda asked.

Selena was desperately trying to get Ethan back. She was in her house, holding the Coffer of Shadow which contained the Omegahedron up toward the mirror and the image of Ethan. The box now weighed a ton. "Power of Shadow, bring him to me!" she ordered. *"You* can do it. You have the power to remove that handsome hunk from Main Street and return him to my house."

The box in her hand glowed hotter. At the same moment on Main Street a giant bulldozer monstrously sprang to life. "Go to it, bulldozer!" Selena commanded. "Scoop him up for me."

The bulldozer crashed through a fence near Ethan. No one was at the controls. Belching black smoke, the giant machine came to life, looking left and right and then spotting Ethan who was frozen in his tracks. Its engine roared as it turned, heading straight for him, its steel jaws snapping. Ethan hid behind a car, but Selena saw him and urged the bulldozer on. Ethan leaped away, just as the giant teeth tore into the roof of the car.

The machine was in pursuit of Ethan. It ran amok, and started to demolish stores, buildings, anything in its path.

Ethan, with the shadow of the machine's gaping teeth hanging over him, desperately tried to run into a building through its double swing doors. But he pushed on the pull side and pulled on the push side. Roar! Crash! The bucket completely tore off the front wall of the building. Then the bulldozer scooped up Ethan and carried him away in its giant steel mouth.

Back at her pink mirror, Selena cheered.

Lucy and Linda were horrified by what they were seeing. Jimmy was trying to take pictures. Lucy ran toward the bulldozer and leaped up into the driver's seat, grabbing onto the controls. "Somebody's got to do something!"

Linda rushed into Popeye's ladies' room at SUPER-SPEED. Moments later, as Supergirl, she surveyed the horrible scene from the roof. The bulldozer was spinning around and around with its occupant, Ethan, in the bucket. The street was alive with electrical discharges from wires. Supergirl zapped the snapping and popping wires with her

SUPER HEAT VISION and then doused a raging fire by flying right through a water tank, releasing its contents. Then Supergirl flew off the water tank in pursuit of the spinning bulldozer. She landed on its bucket, and with a mighty wrench tore it off. The bulldozer came to a halt.

Back in their house, Selena and Bianca were astonished at the sight of Supergirl.

"A Storm Dragon?" Bianca asked.

"No," said Selena. "A super girl."

upergirl flew into a wooded area with the bucket. She landed, walked around the bucket and changed back to Linda Lee. Then effortlessly she pulled the top back and open.

Ethan, covered with soot and debris, stirred. "Ohhh . . ." He opened his eyes and beheld his savior, Linda Lee. It was a moment outside time, this strange girl above him like an angel, looking upon him with such compassion, her tender lips slightly parted. Selena's potion was swimming through Ethan's brain!

Selena and Bianca watched in terrible suspense through the mirror screen. "Don't look at *her!*" Selena yelled.

But it was too late. Ethan's lips moved. Selena and Bianca couldn't hear what he was saying, but it looked like: "I love you."

Linda gazed at Ethan in surprise. "You love me?"

"With all my heart forever!" said Ethan. Gone was that no-nonsense landscaper, the brooding mystery man. Ethan was now an incurable romantic spouting poetry:

> "A bird of free and careless wing
> Was I, through many a smiling spring."

He struggled forward. Linda backed up a bit.

"Stay! Let me behold thee!" said Ethan.

Suddenly his lips were on Linda's. It was her first kiss. Her eyes were wide open but Ethan's were shut tight in reverie.

"I have to . . . I have to . . . *go*," Linda said, prying herself away from Ethan.

Flustered, embarassed and excited, she ran away while Ethan continued to spout romantic poetry.

Selena watched while Linda ran back to Midvale School. "Midvale School!" she said. "Nigel must know her. She must be one of his students. *He* must've put her up to it."

Selena put on her sunglasses, opened the Coffer of Shadow and commanded:

"Power of Shadow, take shape!
Look like a vicious dark star!
Seek out this wretched young creature!
And destroy her wherever she . . . are!"

A black cloud of shadow burst out of the center of the Omegahedron. A huge invisible presence filled the room with darkness and then smashed through the bedroom wall leaving a trail of crushed furniture as it left.

Selena looked around at the violence and destruction. "Next time . . . remind me to do this outside."

In her room at Midvale School Linda thought about her first kiss. She walked toward the mirror and, looking at herself, puckered her lips. There was so much to learn about Earth. The girls talked about so many things that she didn't understand. Streaked hair. Pierced ears. She didn't even know what Memorial Day weekend was. In a way she felt that she belonged here, but in a way she felt she never would. She was so confused.

A horrific crash brought Linda out of her daydreams. She rushed to the window to see the Unseen Monster that Selena had unleashed heading toward her, crushing everything in its path, making the earth tremble. Everything went. A wooden rain shelter, the tennis court, a fence, a car.

Linda took a deep breath, and charged . . . sailing out into the night. Supergirl! The fight began. The huge nightmarish monster flung Supergirl back, trying to crush her with its hideous talons. Lightning was flashing and thunder boom-

ing overhead. Supergirl, breaking off a lamp post at its base, flew up into the storm with it. Huge bolts of lightning struck the lamp post. Supergirl's face contorted with agony as her body absorbed millions and millions of kilowatts. Then, glowing with electricity, she slammed down into the Monster. A tremendous blast of energy . . . crack! The Monster, collapsing in a ghastly rush of dark energy . . . a black hole . . . , shrunk into an evil, shriveled, shapeless lump and shrieked away into the night.

Selena and Bianca had been watching the battle on the mirror screen. "What the devil *is* she?" Selena asked. She was furious.

Bianca tried to reason with her. "Yeah, but I mean you can't go *nuts* because some landscape guy and some teenage kid in a blue suit . . ."

"She *flies!*" screamed Selena. "Can you get that through your thick skull and into your tiny brain, Bianca? The girl can fly!"

Selena opened up a big dusty book to the section "The Rites of Ultimate Power." She concocted some hateful brew according to its directions. She opened the Coffer of Shadow which was getting bigger and bigger and removed the Omegahedron. Everything in the room started to vibrate.

upergirl walked down the empty dorm corridor slowly changing back into Linda. In her room she noticed her bracelet start to glow. Holding the bracelet before her, she followed its lead. When it faded, she retraced her steps until the glow reappeared. It was taking her somewhere, its glow leading the way. It led her to the amusement park, Selena's eerie domain. "We're close, aren't we, Zaltar?" she said to herself.

There was a noise. Using her X-RAY VISION, Linda saw . . . Ethan, hiding behind a carousel and holding a bouquet of red roses and a five-pound heart-shaped box of candy. Still under the sway of Selena's love potion, he had been following Linda.

"Oh, no . . ."

"'Tis only me, my love. Please, at least tell me your name."

"Linda. Linda Lee. But I . . ."

Suddenly Ethan's hands were around Linda's waist as he tried to lift her up onto the carousel. It was heave-ho, but no go.

"What are you doing?" Linda drew back, aware that he wouldn't be able to lift her because of her SUPERWEIGHT.

"Uh, why don't we hop on the carousel, my love," Ethan

suggested, somewhat embarassed. He'd have to start working out again.

Linda, unsure, but drawn toward this earnest, bumbling Romeo, climbed onto the carousel.

Ethan jumped in beside her. "My name is Ethan. Marry me," he beseeched her.

"Ethan, I . . ."

"Don't say it. I know. We're from different worlds."

"You *know*? How?"

"Just give me a chance, Linda. Love makes everything possible. A poor uneducated gardener can indeed worship a rich debutante and make her happy if she just . . ."

Linda, greatly relieved, laughed. "Oh, you mean . . . oh." Linda looked into Ethan's eyes. He was so sincere, so handsome, so sexy. She said, "I'm not rich, Ethan. I'm just not what you think."

"Then I'll support us both."

Linda and Ethan stared into each other's eyes . . . moving closer and closer . . . drawn together like magnets.

"What a touching scene!"

It was Selena, the great sorceress herself, standing at the carousel. She pointed . . . and the carousel instantly started to move, hurling Linda and Ethan back into their seat. Faster and faster! The carousel became a blur. Bianca caught up with Selena just as Selena stopped the ride with a flash of her finger. But only Ethan was aboard.

Then, blasting down from the sky, landing right between Selena and Ethan came Supergirl! "Who are you?" she asked Selena.

"I am Selena! Diodenes of Catania! Priestess of Sekhnet!" Selena said and she gave a list of her titles in alphabetical order.

"And I am Kara of Argo City," Supergirl said. "Daughter of Alura and Zor-El, and I don't scare easily."

"No? Try this on for size."

Selena pointed her finger straight at Ethan and with a flash of light Ethan vanished from the carousel. Dazed and stunned, he reappeared on the platform of the Dodgem Car Ride, where hideously painted cars attacked him. He escaped into one of the cars, but now the other cars were pummeling him.

Supergirl moved forward toward Selena, just as Selena magically duplicated herself. Again and again and again.

Fifty or sixty moving images of Selena encircled Supergirl, forming an impenetrable wall.

Bianca was impressed. "This lady is improving by leaps and bounds, I gotta tell ya."

Supergirl tried to push through the circle. No way. Desperate to help Ethan, she spun around, leaped up and flew out of the circle. Landing in the middle of a pile of tent poles, she snatched up the poles and hurled them at Selena, watching as they buried themselves around Selena, imprisoning her.

Supergirl turned toward Ethan and lifted him and his car up, off into the night sky. This was the second time in twenty-four hours that she had rescued him.

"Where am I? Where is my Linda?" Ethan asked just before a coconut fell out of the sky and bonked him on the head. Supergirl bent over the fallen Ethan. It was morning and Supergirl had flown Ethan to the beach, close to where she had first arrived on Earth.

Selena, having escaped from the encircling poles and once again at home looking through her pink mirror, was making the sky rain coconuts. "That oughta keep her out of my hair for a few hours. But it's just a cheap trick. I still can't control men's minds!"

"So maybe . . . now don't go through the roof . . . but maybe we should, like, back down and give you-know-who a call. You know . . . Nigel," Bianca suggested.

"I'll pretend I didn't hear that."

"All I'm thinking is that he's been *around*. He knows things we don't." Bianca picked up the telephone and boldly extended it to Selena.

Selena contemplated the thought and decided it was time to reach out and touch someone. With not too much coaxing Nigel appeared.

"You must think me a babe in the woods," Nigel said, cautiously, not trusting these two.

"Not at all."

"What's in it for me, Selena?"

"Me . . ."

"Ah . . ." Nigel thought of old times.

Skeptical, but curious, Nigel glanced down at the love potion. "Very interesting," he said, picking up the nutshell and carelessly tossing it in his hands as he spoke, then forgetfully popping open the nutshell and freeing the spider!

"Oops . . . Sorry . . ."

With the spider out, the love potion was null and void.

And back on the beach Ethan was once more himself!

Now he was really confused. He looked up at Supergirl. "Who're you?"

"Kara. From Argo City, daughter of Alura and Zor-El. But you mustn't tell anyone because I'm here on a secret mission."

"Sure you are. Plus on top of that you like to wear Superman's clothes."

"These are *my* clothes. And I have to go now."

Ethan was staring at her. "Linda." Did he know?

"I love Linda," he said. The statement surprised him. "I love Linda?" He tried to shake himself of his confusion. "She was at that amusement park. I have to go back there." Ethan started off.

Supergirl flew over his head and blocked his path.

"You just flew over my head, didn't you?" he said. "Like Superman."

"He's my cousin. I shouldn't be telling you all this. I'm here under cover . . ."

"You can do the whole number, right? Leap tall buildings at a single bound? Look right through things? Bend steel bars?"

"Yes, but I have to go. Selena has the Omegahedron."

"Take me with you. I have to find Linda. I *love* her."

They were inches apart, staring into each other's eyes.

Back at Selena's house things were heating up. Selena was luring Nigel into helping her.

"And the first thing we have to do is get rid of Supergirl."

"How?"

"By getting *him*. She'll follow."

"And then check out of this dump, I hope," Bianca added.

"Well, Nigel . . . are we in business?" Selena asked.

"Oh, indeed. But I need the little mystery ball . . ."

Selena was reluctant, holding on in a kind of tug-of-war with Nigel over the Omegahedron. But whamo! Out of his attaché case Nigel took the Burundiwand, a twisted, tortured bone hung with monkey feet and feathers—an object of pure unadulterated evil. And as Nigel brought the Burundiwand to the Omegahedron, just as Zaltar had brought his Matterwand to it, the Burundiwand crackled to life. And the Omegahedron zapped all about, Selena clinging onto it for dear life.

The mirror flashed and went static, filling with electronic distortions and rolling images, all the usual symptoms of a failing picture tube . . . before it found Supergirl and Ethan on the beach.

"How can you love her? You don't even know her," Supergirl was saying.

Ethan replied, "Oh, yes, I do. And I have to go to her."

"Linda is *not* in trouble," Supergirl said.

But Supergirl was. She was falling for Ethan, this handsome, sincere, desperately romantic earthling. But just as Supergirl leaned toward Ethan and kissed him there was a blast of light and Ethan was gone!

Another blast of light and Selena now had Ethan chained on top of her huge bed. It had worked. Supergirl stood in the pink mirror alone.

Nigel was pleased, but not for long. Selena had duped him and the good times were not ahead, as Selena touched the Burundiwand to the Omegahedron and transformed Nigel into—an old man!

Supergirl, with a look of fierce determination, flew to the intersection of Main and Broadway in Midvale where a most amazing sight greeted her. A ghastly, craggy mountain now towered insanely over the city, its base taking up the

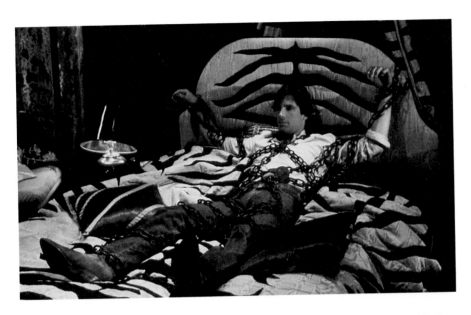

entire intersection. Angry motorists honked their horns; traffic was hopelessly snarled. People all around were stopped in their tracks, staring and pointing.

Whoosh! Supergirl, after taking in all the madness below, landed on the peak of the hideous mountain. There sat the most fantastic new house, a spectacularly elegant, imposing mansion, but forbiding in its starkness and bareness. With a graceful bound, Supergirl landed on the balcony of the house and warily stepped inside the french doors, her attention first caught by the statue of a grotesque demon perched on a beam, silhouetted against the windows. And there at the end of the room, chained across a huge fireplace, helpless, his eyes staring widely, desperately up at her was Ethan!

Supergirl ran toward him but before she could reach him a polygon appeared seemingly out of nowhere. IT WAS A DOOR TO THE PHANTOM ZONE! And Supergirl was trapped within it.

"Got her!" said Selena, suddenly materializing at Ethan's side, laughing. She gestured with the Burundiwand, and Ethan's chains fell away. Ethan looked blankly at Supergirl trapped behind the shimmering polygon. Supergirl tried to call out to Ethan, her hands and face pressed against the transparent walls of the polygon. "Ethan! Don't let her do this!" But not even a cry of anguish could escape the impenetrable force-field.

"Enjoy your prison, Supergirl. Forever and ever," Selena said as she kissed Ethan with fierce lust. He returned it with great emotion as their images began to recede and Supergirl's prison whirled away into darkness.

Supergirl found herself in the Phantom Zone. Her crystal prison landed and shattered, and she confronted a strange, alien, slimy, lifeless landscape. She picked herself up from the fragments of her prison and raised her arms to fly. BUT SHE COULDN'T FLY! She picked up a small rock and tried to crush it in her hand. IT WAS IMPOSSIBLE! She scooped up some sand, cupped it in her palm and tried to blow it away. SHE COULDN'T DO IT! Her powers were gone!

Supergirl started to walk, a tiny figure, trudging onward, exhausted, despairing, her once-gorgeous hair unkempt, streaks of dirt and grit on her sweaty face. But where was she walking to? She was lost in a vast, hellish limbo that seemed never to have been inhabited by a living creature. It was an endless prison with her as the sole wretched occupant.

She stumbled and fell unconscious. When she awoke she was in a filthy dome-like dwelling, walls wet with algae, the floor slippery, some sort of vicious slime dripping from its stalactite ceiling. She was on some dirty blankets, and there was a man taking care of her. She recognized him. "Zaltar!"

He had changed. Oh, how he had changed. He was a frightful sight, dissipated, haggard, all the fire and energy drained away.

"Zaltar," she said, "it's me, Kara."

"I know," he said, and he gave her something to drink.

"Where are we?"

"Nowhere."

"The Phantom Zone!"

"I have been here forever and here I shall stay forever. And now, dear Kara, I'm afraid you're doomed here also."

"No. We have to get to Earth, Zaltar, and get the Omega-hedron and take it back to Argo City. A wicked sorceress has the Power Source. She sent me here. She's as powerful as the Guardians, but she is evil and the Guardians are good."

"And Zaltar is *bad*," said Zaltar.

"Self-pity? You always taught me to have pride, Zaltar. And you just can't give up! You founded a whole *city!*"

"And then doomed it to destruction."

Supergirl looked around. "What's this?" she asked. "Why, it's a tiny mud sculpture. You made this here. Then you *haven't* given up. We can get to Earth together. There must be a way out of here."

"There is one. But we could die trying."

"We won't!"

"You have to confront the Maelstrom to prevail. You have to enter the Quantum Vortex. Gigantic storms, sheer walls . . . it's horrifying. But if you have the courage, come."

Zaltar led Supergirl into the howling, swirling walls which sloped upward toward a bright light. The Maelstrom below tried to suck them back. Zaltar slipped. Supergirl grabbed his hand and kept him from the Maelstrom screaming below. Using her determination and will, she climbed higher, an inspiration to Zaltar. They were almost to the top.

On Earth, in Midvale, Selena was in full power. Four motorcycle cops whose faces were completely covered by dark, reflecting helmets led her and Bianca in their police-chauffeured Rolls-Royce through the streets. Ethan, beside Selena, stared vacantly into space. Nigel was in back. Ordinary citizens scurried into doorways in fear of this procession. Only Lucy Lane stepped out into the street, daring to defy Selena. But Selena had plans for her and her friend Jimmy Olsen. Hideous plans.

Back at her mansion, Selena made a gesture, and a chandelier of sorts appeared. It was composed of four giant cages, one containing Lucy Lane, another Jimmy Olsen, the third the old man Nigel, and the fourth ominously empty.

"I woulda thought, myself, maybe a ceiling fan, but it's your house," said Bianca.

Selena felt triumphant. Today Midvale, tomorrow the world, and the day after tomorrow, the universe!

But something was wrong. The Coffer of Shadow jumped open of its own accord. The reflecting surface of the pink mirror was turning on. In view, escaping from the Phantom Zone, was a man and Supergirl.

"Curses!" said Selena. "How do you murder someone in the Phantom Zone?"

A gigantic, monstrous shadow-being hovered behind Selena as she remotely hurled Thessalian Fireballs at Supergirl and Zaltar.

Zaltar was hit. He was knocked off the wall and started to tumble down the vortex. But Supergirl reached for him, hooked his fingertips, and Zaltar wedged himself between Supergirl and the howling funnel cloud, sheltering Supergirl. But again he started to roll backward down the vortex.

"Zaltar!" Supergirl cried.

"Higher . . . go higher!"

"Come with me!"

"Yes. Of course."

But Supergirl looked back to see Zaltar's fingers torn from the rock and his body sucked backward into the funnel cloud and swept out of sight. "Zaltar! No!"

Supergirl, sadly, but with enormous resolve, ducked another fireball and resumed her climb. Closer and closer to that light atop the vortex, only yards away . . . closer . . . CRACK! She charged the hot, glowing orb.

Supergirl blasted right through Selena's pink mirror, flying like a speeding bullet, shattering glass in every direction. "You've had your fun, Selena. The game is over."

"Hardly. One false step, blue bird, and your friends'll get the point." Selena pointed to the cages suspended from the ceiling . . . directly over huge lethal spikes, seemingly growing right out of the floor. Red hot and glowing. Selena gestured to the cages and the chains snapped.

Supergirl exhaled. SUPER ICY BREATH that swept across the steaming hot spikes, freezing them to the point where they exploded. The cages smashed to the floor and as the smoke cleared, Lucy, Jimmy and Nigel ran to safety.

Supergirl faced Selena. "I want the Omegahedron."

"Well, then, Supergirl, you shall have it."

Selena opened the lid of the grotesquely swollen Coffer of Shadow. The Omegahedron spun and glittered inside, releasing a gale-force wind that swept through the room and launched itself at Supergirl. The brick wall behind Supergirl started to heave, then bulged out and crashed down on Supergirl, engulfing her in its debris.

From below, the room began to undulate and flames and smoke erupted. Supergirl struggled to keep her balance over the hellfire underneath while a demon statue dangled precariously above her.

"Supergirl! Above you! Look out!" Ethan cried. He seemed to be changing sides.

Supergirl leaped to one side as the demon statue crashed into the fury below, enveloping the room in a blinding flash and a huge, smoky explosion.

Selena's eyes turned bright orange. Chanting and raving, she lifted her arms and her astral image—that beast appearing from time to time—emerged out of the dense black mist. It was her shadow self, mimicking and reflecting her every gesture.

"Power of Shadow, destroy Supergirl!" As Selena raised her hands so did the beast, this hideous extension of herself.

Supergirl leaped onto a beam overhead but the beast, manipulated by the raging, unrelenting sorceress, lunged across the room after her. Closing on her with its gigantic taloned claws, the beast entwined itself with Supergirl in a deadly midair struggle, stretching, twisting, distorting Supergirl hopelessly out of shape. It was a nightmarish sight.

Supergirl's resistance was at its lowest ebb. But suddenly she heard the echo of Zaltar's voice, "I am with you . . . go on, girl," and she summoned every ounce of remaining strength. She pulled herself into a crouching position, coiled like a spring and flipped backward in a blinding flash, bursting free from the demon's grip.

"Make her confront it! It's the only way!" Nigel warned Supergirl.

Supergirl looked desperately at the horrific sight of Selena, white as death, eyes transfixed, body shaking. She had to find a way to deal with this raging madwoman. And then Ethan crawled to the Coffer of Shadow and slammed the lid, giving Supergirl her break: Selena had lost access to the power of the Omegahedron.

At SUPERSPEED, Supergirl caught Selena and thrust her upward in a spiral of smoke so that she faced her own beast. Continuing her flying spin around the sorceress and her beast, Supergirl whirled a cyclone which she guided across the room toward the smoking hole that was Selena's mirror. As the tip of the cyclone caught in the mirror, Selena was swept head first through the empty pink frame and into the Quantum Vortex beyond. She was gone! Then a great wind, beckoning from the vortex, pulled Bianca toward the pink-framed abyss.

"No . . . no . . . there's a serious misunderstanding here," Bianca explained as she was lifted off the floor and sucked against the opening. "I just *worked* for her! I only did what I was . . ."

Bianca was gone, too. The scattered fragments of the mirror rose from the floor and the mirror reassembled itself, once again whole.

Lucy, Jimmy and Nigel emerged from their hiding places, stunned and shaken but impressed by what they had just seen. Nigel walked toward the pink mirror and gazed at it, sadly.

"I have to go, to return this where it belongs," Supergirl said looking at the Omegahedron. "And I have to ask you all something."

"You don't have to, Supergirl," Jimmy interrupted her. "It's okay. We never saw a thing."

"We never even heard of you," Lucy piped in.

Supergirl turned to Ethan and took his hand, hesitantly. "Ethan, Linda had to leave . . . in a hurry. But I know that she . . ."

Ethan smiled back at her, understanding. "I know. It's alright. You don't have to explain. Well . . . take care of yourself, kiddo."

"You, too, Ethan." She touched her fingertips to his lips, briefly and gently.

Midvale was back to normal. The mountain was gone from the intersection of Main and Broadway. Lucy and Jimmy were there, kissing as if it had only just been invented.

Ethan was alone on the corner. A wistful, longing look

crossed his face. He looked upward into the sky at a disappearing blue streak. "Goodbye, Linda. . . ."

Supergirl flew faster than a speeding bullet, the Omegahedron in her hand, the glowing bracelet at her wrist. Diving from the sky into the green ocean waters, the world around her darkening, Supergirl found her path lighted by the intense glow of the Omegahedron.

At last, speeding past earth and away into the galaxies, Supergirl spotted the great dome of Argo City. It was so much darker than before, though, alarmingly dim.

But the great dome suddenly began to brighten! Brighter and brighter it got as Supergirl got closer, taking the glorious Omegahedron back home!

Argo City would ever again be a glowing jewel in the darkness of Inner Space.